HOW MANY BEARS?

HOW MANY BEARS?

by **COOPER EDENS**

illustrated by **MARJETT SCHILLE**

ATHENEUM 1994 NEW YORK

Maxwell Macmillan Canada
Toronto
Maxwell Macmillan International
New York Oxford Singapore Sydney

Atheneum
Macmillan Publishing Company
866 Third Avenue
New York, NY 10022

Maxwell Macmillan Canada, Inc.
1200 Eglinton Avenue East
Suite 200
Don Mills, Ontario M3C 3N1

Macmillan Publishing Company is part of the
Maxwell Communication Group of Companies.

First edition
Printed in the United States of America on recycled paper
10   9   8   7   6   5   4   3   2   1
The text of this book is set in 14 point Clearface.
The illustrations are rendered in watercolors.

Library of Congress Cataloging-in-Publication Data

Edens, Cooper.
How many bears? / by Cooper Edens ; illustrated by Marjett C.
Schille.—1st ed.
p.   cm.
ISBN 0-689-31923-1
1. Arithmetic—Juvenile literature. [1. Arithmetic.]
I. Schille, Marjett C., ill.   II. Title.
QA115.E34   1994
513.2—dc20   94-9371

For Willi and Tory
—C. E.

For Emmett E. Schille
—M. S.

Welcome to Little Animal Town, an unusual town indeed, where each morning the town's residents open their shops and invite you to come inside.

Please stop in and take a look. Besides all the things they have to sell, the little animals have a challenge for you. Can you figure out:

How many Bears it takes to run the Bakery in Little Animal Town?

You'll visit that shop last, but each shop along the way has some clues for you. First count the animals who run each shop (only the real ones, don't be fooled), then read the clue on the opposite page. The rest is up to you.

In Little Animal Town…it takes four fewer Giraffes to run the Soda
Fountain than it takes Bears to run the Bakery,

twice as many Tigers to run the Candy Counter,

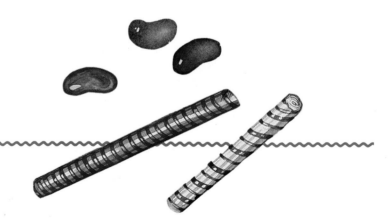

one more Kangaroo to run the Newsstand,

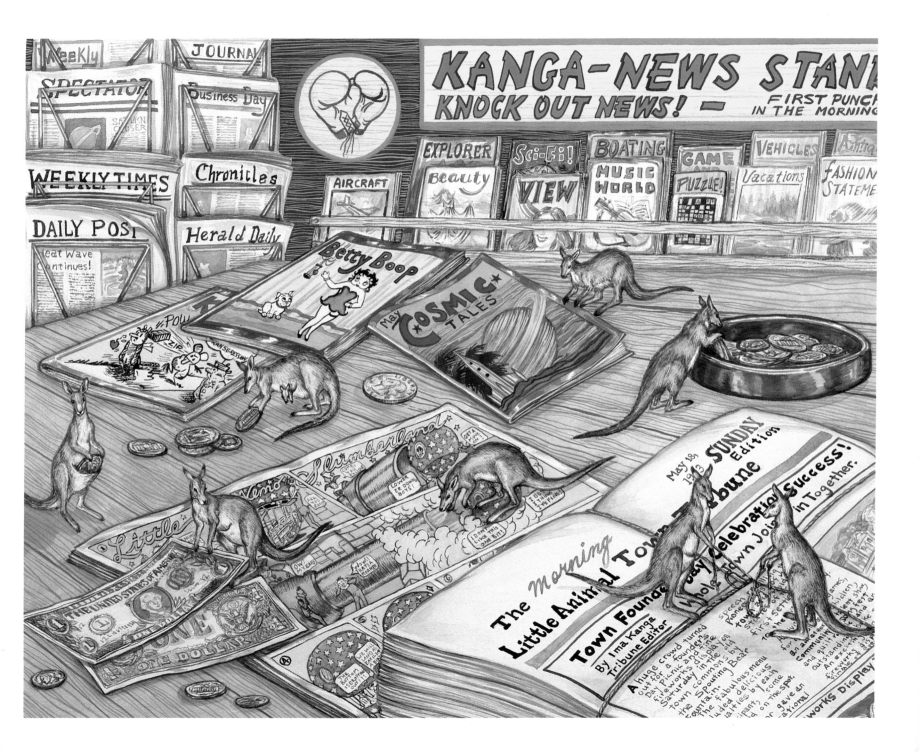

but one Walrus fewer to run the Post Office.

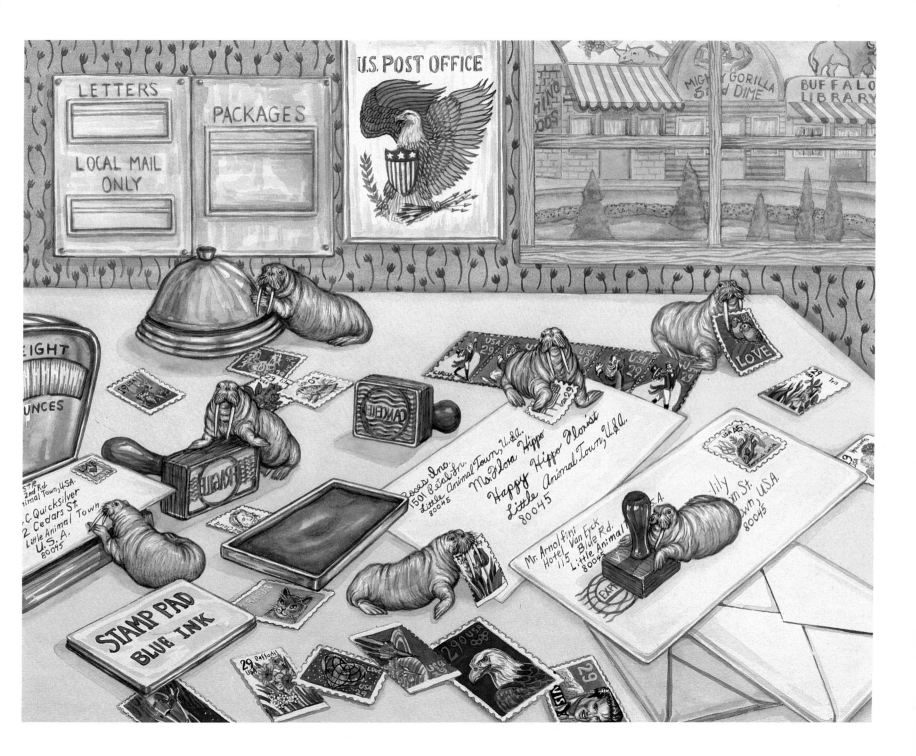

Do you know the answer yet? Keep counting the animals and read along. You'll have the answer soon.

In Little Animal Town...it takes three times as many Gorillas to run the Five and Dime,

two more Buffalo to run the Library,

two fewer Rhinos to run the Grocery,

four times as many Hippos to run the Flower Shop,

three more Elephants to run the Music Store,

and three fewer Alligators to run the Beauty Parlor, than it takes Bears to run the Bakery.

Now you've had time to take a look at all the clues. You have answered the question correctly if you have found it takes eight Bears to run the Bakery in Little Animal Town.

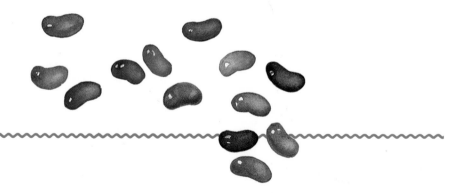

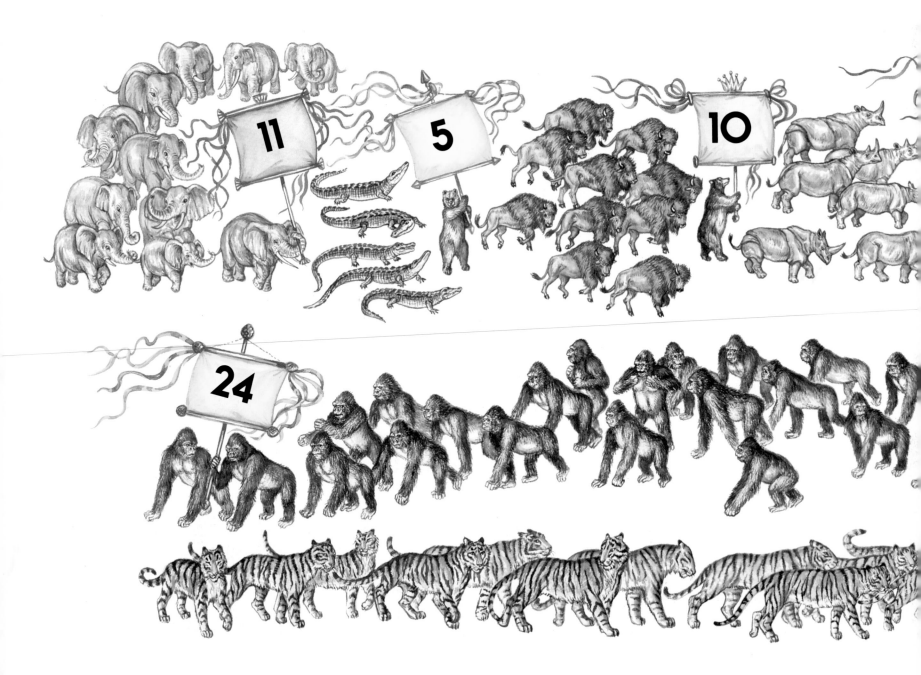

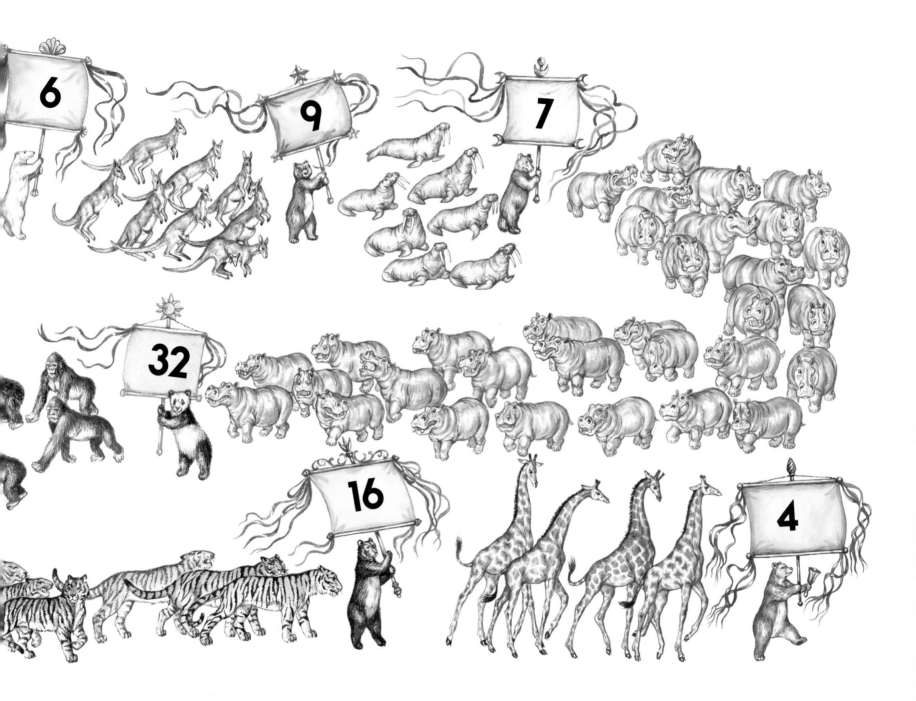

Now that you know how many Bears it takes to run the Bakery in Little Animal Town, perhaps you'd like to test your skill with some other challenges these animals have for you.

CHALLENGE 1

As you know, each shop in Little Animal Town is run by a particular number of animals.
So... what shop would you be in if:
1) There are twice as many animals as there are Tigers?
2) There are four more animals than there are Walruses?
3) There is one animal fewer than there are Alligators?
4) There are four times as many animals as there are Rhinos?
5) There is one more animal than there are Kangaroos?

CHALLENGE 2

Every afternoon one animal from each shop stops by the Bakery to buy a snack for the animals in each shop to share. Chocolate-chip cookies are the Bears' specialty.
How many cookies would each animal get if:
A) The Giraffes shared twelve cookies?
B) The Buffalo shared fifty cookies?
C) The Alligators shared thirty cookies?
D) The Rhinos shared twenty-four cookies?